James T. DeShields

Cynthia Ann Parker

The Story of her Capture

James T. DeShields

Cynthia Ann Parker
The Story of her Capture

ISBN/EAN: 9783743400092

Manufactured in Europe, USA, Canada, Australia, Japa

Cover: Foto ©Raphael Reischuk / pixelio.de

Manufactured and distributed by brebook publishing software
(www.brebook.com)

James T. DeShields

Cynthia Ann Parker

CYNTHIA ANN PARKER.

THE STORY OF HER CAPTURE

At the Massacre of the Inmates of Parker's Fort; of her Quarter of a Century
Spent Among the Comanches, as the Wife of the War Chief, Peta No-
cona; and of her Recapture at the Battle of Pease River, by
Captain L. S. Ross, of the Texian Rangers.

— BY —

JAMES T. DeSHIELDS,

Author of "Frontier Sketches," Etc.

"Truth is Stranger than Fiction."

ILLUSTRATED.

ST. LOUIS:
Printed for the Author,
1886.

CHAS. B. WOODWARD
Printing and Book Manufacturing Co.,
ST. LOUIS.

DEDICATED

(By Permission)

— TO —

GENL. L. S. ROSS,

— OF —

WACO, TEXAS.

PREFACE.

In the month of June, 1884, there appeared in the columns of the Forth Worth *Gazette* an advertisement signed by the Comanche chief, Quanah Parker, and dated from the reservation near Fort Sill, in the Indian Territory, enquiring for a photograph of his late mother, Cynthia Ann Parker, which served to revive interest in a tragedy which has always been enveloped in a greater degree of mournful romance and pathos than any of the soul-stirring episodes of our pioneer life, so fruitful of incidents of an adventurous nature.

From the valued narratives kindly furnished us by Victor M. Ross, Major John Henry Brown, and Gen. L. S. Ross, supplemented by the Jas. W. Parker book and copious notes from Hon. Ben. F. Parker, together with most of the numerous partial accounts of the fall of Parker's Fort and subsequent relative events, published during the past fifty years; and after a careful investigation and study of the whole, we have laboriously and with much pains-taking, sifted out and evolved the foregoing narrative of plain, unvarnished facts, which form a part of the romantic history of Texas.

In the preparation of our little volume the thanks of the youthful author are due to Gen. L. S. Ross, of

Waco; Major John Henry Brown of Dallas; Gen. Walter P. Lane of Marshall; Col. John S. Ford of San Antonio; Rev. Homer S. Thrall—the eminent historian of Texas; Mr. A. F. Corning of Waco; Capt. Lee Hall, Indian Agent, I. T., and Mrs. C. A. Westbrook of Lorena, for valuable assistance rendered.

To Victor M. Ross of Laredo, Texas, the author has been placed under many and lasting obligations for valuable data so generously placed at his disposal, and that too at considerable sacrifice to the donor.

From this source we have obtained much of the matter for our narrative.

In submitting our little work—the first efforts of the youthful author—we assure the reader that while there are, doubtless, many defects and imperfections, he is not reading fiction, but facts which form only a part of the tragic and romantic history of the Lone Star State.

JAMES T. DeSHIELDS,

BELTON, Texas, May 19, 1886.

CONTENTS.

CYNTHIA ANN PARKER.

CHAPTER I.

The Parker Fort Massacre, Etc.

CONTEMPORARY with, and among the earliest of the daring and hardy pioneers that penetrated the eastern portion of the Mexican province of Texas, were the "Parker family," who immigrated from Cole county, Illinois, in the fall of the year 1833, settling on the west side of the Navasota creek, near the site of the present town of Groesbeck, in Limestone county, one or two of the family coming a little earlier and some a little later.

The elder John Parker was a native of Virginia, resided for a time in Elbert county, Georgia, but chiefly reared his family in Bedford county, Tennessee, whence in 1818 he removed to Illinois.

The family, with perhaps one or two exceptions, belonged to one branch of the primitive Baptist church, commonly designated as "two seed," or "hard shell" Baptists.

In the spring of 1834 the colonist erected Parker's Fort, [1]) a kind of wooden barricade, or wall around their cabins, which served as a means of better protecting themselves against the numerous predatory bands of Indians into that, then, sparsely settled section.

As early as 1829 the "Prairie Indians" had declared war against the settlers, and were now actively hostile,

---

1) The reader will understand by this term, not only a place of defense, but the residence of a small number of families belonging to the same neighborhood. As the Indian mode of warfare was an indiscriminate slaughter of all ages, and both sexes, it was as requisite to provide for the safety of the women and children as for that of the men.

Dodridge's faithful pen picture of early pioneer forts, will perhaps give the reader a glimps of old Fort Parker in the dark and bloody period of its existence. He says:

"The *fort* consisted of cabins, blockhouses, and stockades. A range of cabins commonly formed on one side at least of the fort. Divisions, or portions of logs, separated the cabins from each other. The walls on the outside were ten or twelve feet high, the slope of the roof being turned wholly inward. A very few of these cabins had puncheon floors, the greater part were earthen. The blockhouses were built at the angles of the fort. They projected about two feet beyond the outer walls of the cabins and stockades. Their upper stories were about eighteen inches every way larger in dimension than the under one, leaving an opening at the commencement of the second to prevent the enemy from making a lodgment under their walls. In some forts, instead of blockhouses the angles of the fort were furnished with bastions. A large folding gate, made of thick slabs, nearest the spring, closed the fort. The stockades, bastions, cabins, and blockhouse walls, were furnished with port-holes at proper heights and distances. The whole of the outside was completely bullet-proof.

It may be truly said that "necessity is the mother of invention"; for the whole of this work was made without the aid of a single nail or spike of iron; and for this reason such things were not to be had. In some places, less exposed, a single blockhouse, with a cabin or two, constituted the whole fort. Such places of refuge may appear very trifling to those who have been in the habit of seeing the formidable military garrisons of Europe and America, but they answered the purpose, as the Indians had no artillery. They seldom attacked, and scarcely ever took one of them."

constantly committing depredations in different localities.

Parker's colony at this time consisted of only some
eight or nine families, viz: Elder John Parker, patriarch of the family, and his wife; his son James W.
Parker, wife, four single children and his daughter,
Mrs. Rachel Plummer, her husband, L. M. T. Plummer, and infant son, fifteen months old; Mrs. Sarah
Nixon, another daughter, and her husband L. D.
Nixon; Silas M. Parker (another son of Elder John),
his wife and four children; Benjamin F. Parker, an
unmarried son of the Elder [2]); Mrs. Nixon, sr.,
mother of Mrs. James W. Parker; Mrs. Elizabeth
Kellogg, daughter of Mrs. Nixon; Mrs. —— Duty;
Samuel M. Frost, wife and two children; G. E.
Dwight, wife and two children; in all thirty-four persons.

Besides those above mentioned, old man—— Lunn,
David Faulkenberry and his son Evan, Silas Bates,
and Abram Anglin, a boy, had erected cabins a mile
or two distant from the fort, where they resided.

---

2) Elder Daniel Parker, a man of strong mental powers, a son of
Elder John, does not figure in these events. He signed the Declaration
of Independence in 1836, and preached to his people till his death in
Anderson county in 1845. Ex-Representative Ben. F. Parker, is his son
and successor in preaching at the same place. Isaac Parker, above mentioned, another son, long represented Houston and Anderson counties in
Senate and House, and in 1855 represented Tarrant county. He died in
Parker county, not long since, not far from 88 years of age. Isaac D.
Parker of Tarrant is his son.

These families were truly the advance guard of civilization of that part of our frontier. Fort Houston, in Anderson county, being the nearest protection, except their own trusty rifles.

Here the struggling colonist remained, engaged in the avocations of a rural life, tilling the soil, hunting buffalo, bear, deer, turkeys and smaller game, which served abundantly to supply their larder at all times with fresh meat, in the enjoyment of a life of Arcadian simplicity, virtue and contentment, until the latter part of the year 1835, when the Indians and Mexicans forced the little band of compatriots to abandon their homes, and flee with many others before the invading army from Mexico.

On arriving at the Trinity river they were compelled to halt in consequence of an overflow. Before they could cross the swollen stream the sudden and unexpected news reached them that Santa Anna and his vandal hordes had been confronted and defeated at San Jacinto, that sanguinary engagement which gave birth to the new sovereignty of Texas, and that TEXAS WAS FREE FROM MEXICAN TYRANNY.

On receipt of this news the fleeing settlers were overjoyed, and at once returned to their abandoned homes.

The Parker colony now retraced their steps, first going to Fort Houston, where they remained a few days in order to procure supplies, after which they made their way back to Fort Parker to look after their stock and to prepare for a crop.

These hardy sons of toil spent their nights in the fort, repairing to their farms early each morning.

On the night of May 18, 1836, all slept at the fort, James W. Parker, Nixon and Plummer repairing to their field a mile distant on the Navasota, early next morning, little thinking of the great calamity that was soon to befall them.

About 9 o'clock a. m. the fort was visited by several hundred[3]) Comanche and Kiowa Indians. On approaching to within about three hundred yards of the fort the Indians halted in the prairie, presenting a white flag; at the same time making signs of friendship.

At this time there were only six men in the fort, three having gone out to work in the field as above stated. Of the six men remaining, only five were able to bear arms, viz: Elder John Parker, Benjamin and Silas Parker, Samuel and Robert Frost. There were ten women and fifteen children.

The Indians, artfully feigning the treacherous semblance of friendship, pretented that they were looking for a suitable camping place, and enquired as to the exact

---

3) Different accounts have variously estimated the number of Indians at from 300 to 700. One account says 300, another 500, and still another 700. There were perhaps about 500 warriors.

locality of a water-hole in the vicinity, at the same time asking for a beef to appease their hungry—a want always felt by an Indian, when the promise of fresh meat loomed up in the distant perspective; and he would make such pleas with all the servile sicophancy of a slave, like the Italian who embraces his victim ere plunging the poniard into his heart.

Not daring to resent so formidable a body of savages, or refuse to comply with their requests, Mr. Benjamin F. Parker went out to them, had a talk and returned, expressing the opinion that the Indians were hostile and intented to fight, but added that he would go back and try to avert it. His brother Silas remonstrated, but he persisted in going, and was immediately surrounded and killed, whereupon the whole force—their savage instincts aroused by the sight of blood—charged upon the works, uttering the most terrific and unearthly yells that ever greeted the ears of mortals. Cries and confusion reigned. The sickening and bloody tragedy was soon enacted. Brave Silas M. Parker fell on the outside of the fort, while he was gallantly fighting to save Mrs. Plummer. Mrs. Plummer made a most manful resistance, but was soon overpowered, knocked down with a hoe and made captive. Samuel M. Frost and his son Robert met their fate while heroically defending the women and children inside the stockade. Old Granny Parker was outraged, stabbed and left for dead. Elder John Parker, wife and Mrs. Kellogg attempted to make their escape, and in the effort had gone about three-fourths of a mile, when they were overtaken and driven back near to the fort where the old gentleman was stripped, murdered, scalped and horribly mutilated. Mrs. Parker was stripped, speared and left for dead, but by feigning death escaped, as will be seen further on. Mrs. Kellogg was spared as a captive.

The result summed up, was as follows:

Killed—Elder John Parker, aged seventy-nine; Silas M. and Benjamin F. Parker; Samuel M. and his son Robert Frost.

Wounded dangerously—Mrs. John Parker; Old Granny Parker and Mrs.——Duty.

Captured—Mrs. Rachel Plummer, (daughter of James W. Parker), and her son James Pratt Plummer, two years of age; Mrs. Elizabeth Kellogg; Cynthia Ann Parker, nine years old, and her little brother John Parker, aged six years, children of Silas M. Parker. The remainder of the inmates making their escape, as we shall narrate.

When the attack on the fort first commenced, Mrs. Sarah Nixon made her escape and hastened to the field to advise her father, husband and Plummer. On her arrival, Plummer hurried on horseback to inform the Faulkenberrys, Lunn, Bates and Anglin. Parker and Nixon started to the fort, but the former met his family on the way, and carried them some five miles down the Navasota, secreting them in the bottom. Nixon, though unarmed, continued on towards the fort, and met Mrs. Lucy, wife of the dead Silas Parker, with her four children, just as they were intercepted by a small party of mounted and foot Indians. They compelled the mother to lift behind two mounted warriors her daughter Cynthia Ann, and her little son John. The foot Indians now took Mrs. Parker, her two youngest children and Nixon back to the fort.

Just as the Indians were about to kill Nixon, David Faulkenberry appeared with his rifle, and caused them to fall back. Nixon, after his narrow escape from death, seemed very much excited, and immediately left in search of his wife, soon falling in with Dwight, with his own and Frost's family. Dwight and party soon overtook J. W. Parker and went with him to the hiding place in the bottom.

Faulkenberry, thus left with Mrs. Parker and her two children, bade her to follow him. With the infant in her arms and leading the other child she obeyed. Seeing them leave the fort, the Indians made several feints, but were held in check by the brave man's rifle. Several mounted warriors, armed with bows and arrows strung and drawn, and with terrific yells would charge them, but as Faulkenberry would present his gun they would halt, throw up their shields, right about, wheel and retire to a safe distance. This continued for some distance, until they had passed through a prairie of some forty or fifty acres. Just as they were entering the woods, the Indians made a desperate charge, when one warrior, more daring than the others, dashed up so near that Mrs. Parker's faithful dog seized his horse by the nose, whereupon both horse and rider somersaulted, alighting on their backs in a ravine. Just at this moment Silas Bates, Abram Anglin and Evan Faulkenberry, armed, and Plummer unarmed, came up, causing the Indians to retire, after which the party made their way unmolested.

As they were passing through the field where the three men had been at work in the morning, Plummer, as if aroused from a dream, demanded to know what had become of his wife and child. Armed only with a butcher knife, he left the party, in search of his loved ones, and was seen no more for six days.

The Faulkenberrys, Lunn, with Mrs. Parker and children, secreted themselves in a small creek bottom, some distance from the first party, each unconcious of the other's whereabouts.

At twilight Abraham Anglin and Evan Faulkenberry started back to the fort to succor the wounded
and those who might have escaped. On their way,
and just as they were passing Faulkenberry's cabin,
Anglin saw his first and only ghost. He says, "It
was dressed in white with long, white hair streaming
down its back. I admit that I was worse scared at
this moment than when the Indians were yelling and
charging us. Seeing me hesitate, my ghost now
beckoned me to come on. Approaching the object it
proved to be old Granny Parker, whom the Indians
had wounded and stripped, with the exception of her
underwear. She had made her way to the house
from the fort by crawling the entire distance. I took
some bed clothing, and carrying her some distance
from the house, made her a bed, covered her up and
left her until we should return from the fort. On arriving at the fort we could not see a single individual
alive or hear a human sound. But the dogs were
barking, the cattle lowing, the horses neighing and
the hogs squealing, making a hideous and strange
meadly of sounds. Mrs. Parker had told me where
she had left some silver, $106.50. This I found
under a hickory bush by moonlight. Finding no one
at the fort we returned to where I had hid Granny
Parker. On taking her up behind me, we made our

way back to our hiding place in the bottom, where we found Nixon, whom we had not seen since his cowardly flight at the time he was rescued by Faulkenberry from the Indians." [4])

On the next morning, Bates, Anglin and E. Faulkenberry went back to the fort to get provisions and horses and to look after the dead. On reaching the fort they found five or six horses, a few saddles and some meal, bacon and honey. Fearing an attack from the red devils who might still be lurking around, they left without burying the dead. Returning to their comrades in the bottom, they all concealed themselves until the next night, when they started through the woods to Fort Houston, which place they reached without material suffering.

Fort Houston, an asylum on this as on many other occasions, stood on what has been for many years the farm of a wise statesman, a chivalrous soldier and a true patriot—John H. Reagan—two miles west of Palestine.

After wandering around and traveling for six days and nights, during which time they suffered much

(4—In the book published by James W. Parker on pages ten and eleven, he states that Nixon liberated Mrs. Parker from the Indians and rescued old Granny Parker. Mr. Anglin, in his account contradicts, or rather corrects this statement. He says: "I positively assert that this is a mistake and I am willing to be qualified to the statement I here make and can prove the same by Silas H. Bates, now living near Graesbeck."

from hunger and thirst, with their clothing torn into shreads, their bodies lacerated with briars and thorns, the women and children with unshod and bleeding feet, the party of James W. Parker ——————— men, and ——————[5]) women and children—reached Tinnin's, at the old San Antonio and Nacogdoches crossing of the Navasota. Being informed of their approach, Messrs. Carter and Courtney, with five horses, met them some miles away, and thus enabled the women and children to ride. The few people around, though but returned to their deserted homes after the victory of San Jacinto, shared all they had of food and clothing with them.

Plummer, after six days of wanderings alone in the wilderness, arrived at the fort the same day.

In due time the members of the party located temporarily as best suited the respective families, most of them returning to Fort Parker soon afterwards.

A burrial party of twelve men from Fort Houston went up and burried the dead. Their remains now repose near the site of old Fort Parker. Peace to their memories. Unadorned are their graves; not even a slab of marble or a memento of any kind has been erected to tell the traveler where rests the remains of this brave little band of pioneer heroes who wrestled with the savage for the mastery of this proud domain.

---

5) We are unable to ascertain the exact number. Different accounts variously estimate the number from 10 to 20.

After the massacre the savages retired with their booty to their own wild haunts amid the hills and valleys of the beautiful Canadian and Pease rivers.

CHAPTER II.

The Captives—Cynthia Ann and John Parker.

Of the captives we will briefly trace their subsequent checkered career.

After leaving the fort the two tribes, the Comanches and Kiowas, remained and traveled together until midnight. They then halted on an open prairie, staked out their horses, placed their pickets, and pitched their camp. Bringing all their prisoners together for the first time, they tied their hands behind them with raw-hide thongs so tightly as to cut the flesh, tied their feet close together, and threw them upon their faces. Then the braves, gathering around with their yet bloody, dripping scalps, commenced their usual war dance. They danced, screamed, yelled, stamping upon their prisoners, beating them with bows until their own blood came near strangling them. The remainder of the night these frail women suffered and had to listen to the cries and groans of their tender little children.

Mrs. Elizabeth Kellogg soon fell into the hands of the Keechis, from whom, six months after her capture, she was purchased by a party of Delawares, who carried her into Nacogdoches and delivered her to

Gen. Houston, who paid them $150.00, the amount they had paid and all they asked.

On the way thence to Fort Houston, escorted by James W. Parker and others, a hostile Indian was slightly wounded and temporarily disabled by a Mr. Smith. Mrs. Kellogg instantly recognized him as the savage who had scalped the patriarch, Elder John Parker, whereupon, without judge, jury or court-martial, or even dallying with " Judge Lynch," he was involentarily hastened to the "happy hunting grounds" of his fathers.

Mrs. Rachel Plummer remained a captive about eighteen months. Soon after her capture she was delivered of a child. The crying of her infant annoyed her captors, and the mother was forced to yield up her offspring to the merciless fiends,—in whose veins the milk of human sympathy had never flowed,—to be murdered before her eyes with all the demoniacal demonstrations of brutality intact in those savages. The innocent little babe but six weeks old was torn madly from the mother's bosom by six giant Indians, one of them clutched the little prattling innocent by the throat, and like a hungry beast with defenseless prey, he held it out in his iron grasp until all evidence of life seemed extinct. Mrs. Plummer's feeble efforts to save her child were utterly fruitless. They tossed it high in the air and repeatedly let it fall on rocks and frozen earth. Supposing the child dead they returned it to its mother, but discovering traces of lingering life, they again, by force, tore it angrily from her, tied plaited ropes around its neck and threw its unprotected body into hedges of prickley pear. They would repeatedly pull it through these lacerating rushes with demonic yells. Finally, they tied the rope attached to its neck to the pommel of a saddle and rode triumphantly around a circuit until it was not only dead but litterly torn to shreds. All that remained of that once beautiful babe was then tossed into the lap of its poor, distracted mother. With an old knife the weeping mother was allowed to dig a grave and bury her babe.

After this she was given as a servant to a very cruel old squaw, who treated her in a most bruatl manner. Her son had been carried off by another party to the far West and she supposed her husband and father had been killed at the massacre. Her infant was dead, and death to her would have been a sweet relief. Life was a burden, and driven almost to desperation, she resolved no longer to submit to the intolerant old squaw. One day when the two were some distance from, although still in sight of the camp, her mistress attempted to beat her with a club. Determined not to submit to this, she wrenched the club from the hands of the squaw and knocked her down. The Indians, who had witnessed the whole proceedings from their camp, now came running up, shouting at the top of their voices. She fully expected to be killed, but they patted her on the shoulder, crying, "Bueno! bueno!!" (Good! good!!) or well done! She now fared much better and soon became a great favorite and was known as the "Fighting Squaw." She was eventually ransomed through the agency of some Mexican Santa Fe traders, by a noble-hearted, American merchant of that place, Mr. William Donahue. She was purchased in the Rocky Mountains so far north of Santa Fe that seventeen days were consumed in reaching that place. She was at once made a member of her benefactor's family, where she received the kindest of care and attention. Ere long she accompanied Mr. and Mrs. Donahue on a visit to Independence, Missouri, where she had the pleasure of meeting and embracing her brother-in-law, L. D. Nixon, and by him was escorted back to her people in Texas.[1]

On the 19th of February, 1838, she reached her father's house, exactly twenty-one months from her

(1—During her stay with the Indians, Mrs. Plummer had many thrilling adventures, which she often related after her reclamation. In narrating her reminiscences, she said that in one of her rambles, after she had been with the Indians some time, she discovered a cave in the mountains, and in company with the old squaw that guarded her, she explored it and found a large diamond, but her mistress immediately demanded it, and she was forced to give it up. She said also here in these mountains she saw a bush which had thorns on it resembling fish-hooks which the Indians used to catch fish with, and she herself has often caught trout with them in the little mountain streams.

capture. She had never seen her little son, James Pratt, since soon after their capture, and knew nothing of his fate. She wrote, or dictated a thrilling and graphic history of her capture and the horrors of her captivity, the tortures and hardships she endured, and all the incidents of her life with her captors, with observations among the savages.[2] In this book she tells the last she saw of Cynthia Ann and John Parker. She died on the 19th of February, 1839, just one year after reaching home. As a remarkable coincidence it may be stated that she was born on the 19th, married on the 19th, captured on the 19th, released on the 19th, reached Independence on the 19th, arrived at home on the 19th, and died on the 19th of the month.

Her son, James Pratt Plummer, after six long and weary years of captivity and suffering, during which time he had lived among many different tribes and traveled several thousand miles, was ransomed and taken to Fort Gibson late in 1842, and reached home in February, 1843, in charge of his grand-father. He

---

(2—This valuable and interesting little book is now *rare, scarce* and *out* of *print*. The full title of the volume is:

"Narration of the Perilous Adventures, miraculous escapes and sufferings of Rev. Jas. W. Parker, during a frontier residence in Texas of fifteen years. With an impartial geographical description of the climate, soil, timber, water, etc., of Texas."—To which is appended the narrative of the capture and subsequent sufferings of Mrs. Rachel Plummer (his daughter) during a captivity of twenty-one months among the Comanche Indians, etc. 18 mo, p. p. 95—35, boards. Louisville, 1844.

became a respected citizen of Anderson county. Both he and his father are now dead.

This still left in captivity Cynthia and John Parker, who, as subsequently learned, were held by separate bands. The brother and sister thus separated, gradually forgot the language, manners and customs of their own people, and became thorough Comanches as the long years stole slowly away. How long the camera of their young brains retained impressions of the old home within the fort, and the loved faces of their pale-faced kindred, no one knows; though it would appear that the fearful massacre should have stamped an impress indellible while life continued. But the young mind, as the twig, is inclined by present circumstances, and often forced in a way wholly foreign to its native and original bent.

John grew up with the little semi-nude Comanche boys of his own age, and played at "hunter" and "warrior" with pop-guns made of the elder stem, or bows and arrows, and often flushed the chaparral for hare and grouse, or entrapped the finny denizens of the mountain brooks with the many peculiar and ingenious devices of the wild man for securing for his repast the toothsome trout which abounds so plentifully in that elevated and delightful region, so long inhabited by the lordly Comanches.

When just arrived at manhood, John accompanied a raiding party down the Rio Grande and into Mexico. Among the captives taken was a young Mexican girl of great beauty, to whom the young warrior felt his heart go out. The affection was reciprocated on the part of the fair Dona Juanita, and the two were soon engaged to be married, so soon as they should arrive at the Comanche village. Each day as the cavalcade moved leisurely, but steadily along, the lovers could be seen riding together, and discussing the anticipated pleasures of connubial life, when suddenly John was prostrated by a violent attack of small-pox. The cavalcade could not tarry, and so it was decided that the poor fellow should be left all alone in the vast *Llano Esticado* to die or recover as fate decreed. But the little Aztec beauty refused to leave her lover, insisting on her captors allowing her to remain and take care of him. To this the Indians reluctantly consented. With Juanita to nurse and cheer him up, John lingered, lived, and ultimately recovered, when, with as little ceremony, perhaps, as consummated the nuptials of the first pair in Eden, they assumed the matrimonial relation; and Dona Juanita's predilections for the customs and comforts of civilization were sufficiently strong to induce her lord to abandon the wild and nomadic life of a savage for the comforts to be found in a straw-thatched *Jackal*. "They settled," says Mr.

Thrall, the historian of Texas, "on a stock ranch in the far West." When the civil war broke out John Parker joined a Mexican company in the Confederate service, and was noted for his gallantry and daring. He, however, refused to leave the soil of Texas, and would, under no circumstances, cross the Sabine into Louisiana. He was still living on his ranch across the Rio Grande a few years ago, but up to that time had never visited any of his relatives in Texas.

Of Cynthia Ann Parker (we will anticipate the thread of the narrative). Four long years have elapsed since she was cruelly torn from a mother's embrace and carried into captivity. During this time no tidings have been recieved of her. Many efforts have been made to ascertain her whereabouts, or fate, but without success; when in 1840, Col. Len. Williams, an old and honored Texian, Mr. —— Stoat, a trader, and a Delaware Indian guide, named "Jack Harry," packed mules with goods and engaged in an expedition of private traffic with the Indians.

On the Canadian river they fell in with Pa-ha-u-ka's band of Comanches, with whom they were peaceably conversant. And with this tribe was Cynthia Ann Parker, who from the day of her capture had never seen a white person. She was then about fourteen years of age and had been with the Indians nearly five years.

Col. Williams found the Indian into whose family she had been adopted, and proposed to redeem her, but the Comanche told him all the goods he had would not ransom her, and at the same time "the fierceness of his countenance," says Col. Williams, "warned me of the danger of further mention of the subject." But old Pa-ha-u-ka prevailed upon him to let them see her. She came and sat down by the root of a tree, and while their presence was doubtless a happy event to the poor stricken captive, who in her doleful captivity had endured everything but death, she refused to speak a word. As she sat there, musing, perhaps, of distant relatives and friends, and the bereavements at the beginning and progress of her distress, they employed every persuasive art to evoke some expression. They told her of her playmates and relatives, and asked what message she would send them, but she had doubtless been commanded to silence, and with no hope or prospect of return was afraid to appear sad or dejected, and by a stoical effort in order to prevent future bad treatment, put the best face possible on the matter. But the anxiety of her mind was betrayed by the perceptible quiver of her lips, showing that she was not insensible to the common feelings of humanity.

As the years rolled by Cynthia Ann speedily developed the charms of womanhood, as with the dusky maidens of her companionship she performed the menial offices of drudgery to which savage custom consigns women,—or practiced those little arts of coquetry maternal to the female heart, whether she be a belle of Madison Square, attired in the most elaborate toilet from the *elite* bazars of Paris, or the half naked savage with matted locks and claw-like nails.

Doubtless the heart of more than one warrior was pierced by the Ulyssean darts from her laughing eyes, or charmed by the silvery ripple of her joyous laughter, and laid at her feet the game taken after a long and arduous chase among the Antelope Hills.

Among the number whom her budding charms brought to her shrine was Peta Nocona, a Comanche war chief, in prowess and renown the peer of the famous and redoubtable "Big Foot," who fell in a desperately contested hand-to-hand encounter with the veteran ranger and Indian fighter, Captain S. P. Ross, now living at Waco, and whose wonderful exploits and deeds of daring furnished themes for song and story at the war dance, the council, and the camp-fire.

Cynthia Ann,—stranger now to every word of her mother tongue save her own name—became the bride of Pata Nocona, performing for her imperious lord all the slavish offices which savageism and Indian custom assigns as the duty of a wife. She bore him children, and we are assured *loved* him with a species of fierce passion, and wifely devotion; "for some fifteen years after her capture," says Victor M. Rose, "a party of white hunters, including some friends of her family, visited the Comanche encampment on the upper Canadian, and recognizing Cynthia Ann—probably through the medium of her name alone, sounded her in a secret manner as to the disagreeableness of a return to her people and the haunts of civilization. She shook her head in a sorrowful negative, and pointed to her little, naked barbarians sporting at her feet, and to the great greasy, lazy buck sleeping in the shade near at hand, the locks of a score of scalps dangling at his belt, and whose first utterance upon arousing would be a stern command to his meek, pale-faced wife. Though in truth, exposure to sun and air had browned the complexion of Cynthia Ann almost as intensely as were those of the native daughters of the plains and forest.

She retained but the vaguest remembrance of her people—as dim and flitting as the phantoms of a dream; she was accustomed now to the wild life she led, and found in its repulsive features charms which "upper tendom" would have proven totally deficient in:—"I am happily wedded," she said to these visitors. "I love my husband, who is good and kind, and my little ones, who, too, are his, and I cannot forsake them!"

* * * * * * * *

What were the incidents in the savage life of these children which in after times became the land marks in the train of memory, and which with civilized creatures serves as incentives to reminiscence?

"Doubtless," says Mr. Rose, "Cynthia Ann arrayed herself in the calico borne from the sacking of Linville, and fled with the discomfited Comanches up the Gaudaloupe and Colorado, at the ruthless march of John II. Moore, Ben McCulloch and their hardy rangers. They must have been present at the battle of Antelope Hills, on the Canadian, when Col. John S. Ford, "Old Rip" and Captain S. P. Ross encountered the whole force of the Comanches, in 1858; perhaps John Parker was an actor in that celebrated battle; and again at the Wichita."

"Their's must have been a hard and unsatisfactory life—the Comanches are veritable Ishmaelites, their hands being raised against all men, and every man's hand against them. Literally, "eternal vigilance was the price of liberty" with them, and of life itself. Every night the dreaded surprise was sought to be guarded against; and every copse was scanned for the anticipated ambuscade while upon the march. Did they flount the blood-drabbled scalps of helpless whites in fiendish glee, and assist at the cruel torture of the unfortunate prisoners that fell into their hands? Alas! forgetful of their race and tongue, they were thorough savages, and acted in all particulars just as their Indian comrades did. Memory was stored but with the hardships and the cruelties of the life about them ; and the stolid indifference of mere animal existence furnishes no finely wrought springs for the rebound of reminiscence.''

*   *   *   *   *   *   *   *

The year 1846, one decade from the fall of Parker's Fort, witnessed the end of the Texian Republic, in whose councils Isaac Parker served as a senator, and the blending of the *Lone Star* with the gallaxy of the great constellation of the American Union ;—during which time many efforts were made to ascertain definitely the whereabouts of the captives, as an indispensable requisite to their reclamation ; sometimes by solitary scouts and spies, sometimes through the medium of negotiation ; and sometimes by waging direct war against their captors,—but all to no avail.

*   *   *   *   *   *   *   *

Another decade passes away, and the year 1856 arrives. The hardy pioneers have pushed the frontier of civilization far to the north and west, driving the Indian and the buffalo before them. The scene of Parker's Fort is now in the heart of a dense population ; farms, towns, churches, and school houses lie along the path by which the Indians marched from their camp at the "water-hole" in that bloody May of 1836.

Isaac Parker is now a Representative in the Legislature of the State of Texas. It is now twenty years since the battle of San Jacinto; twenty years since John and Cynthia Ann were borne into a captivity worse than death; the last gun of the Mexican war rung out its last report over the conquered capital of Mexico ten long years ago; but John and Cynthia Ann Parker have sent no tokens to their so long anxious friends that they even live: Alas! time even blunts the edge of anxiety, and sets bounds alike to the anguish of man, as well as to his hopes.

The punishment of Prometheas is not of this world!

CHAPTER III.

The Battle of Antelope Hills.

"Brave Colonel Ford the commander and ranger bold,
  On the South Canadian did the Comanches behold,
On the 12th of May, at rising of sun,
  The armies did meet and the battle begun."

The battle of the South Canadian or "Antelope
Hills," fought in 1858, was probably one of the most
splendid scenic exhibitions of Indian warfare ever enacted upon Texas soil.   This was the immemorial
home of the Comanches ; here they sought refuge from
their marauding expeditions into Texas and Mexico ;
and here, in their veritable "city of refuge," should
the adventurous and daring rangers seek them, it was
certain that they would be encountered in full force—
Pohebits Quasho—"Iron Jacket," so called from the
fact that he wore a coat of scale mail, a curious piece
of ancient armor, which doubtless had been stripped
from the body of some unfortunate Spanish Knight
slain, perhaps, a century before—some chevalier who
followed Coronado, De Leon, La Salle—was the war
chief.   He was a "Big Medicine" man, or Prophet,
and claimed to be invulnerable to balls and arrows
aimed at his person, as by a necromantic puff of his
breath the missives were diverted from their course, or
charmed, and made to fall harmless at his feet.

Peta Nocono, the young and daring husband of Cynthia Ann Parker, was second in command.

About the 1st of May, in the year above named, Col. John S. Ford, ("Old Rip,") at the head of 100 Texian Rangers—comprising such leaders as Capts. S. P. Ross, (the father of Gen. L. S. Ross) ; W. A. Pitts, Preston, Tankersley, and a contingent of 111 Toncahua Indians, the latter commanded by their celebrated chief, Placido—so long the faithful and implicitly trusted friend of the whites—marched on a campaign against the maruding Comanches, determined to follow them up to their stronghold amid the hills of the Canadian river, and if possible surprise them and inflict a severe and lasting chastisement.

After a toilsome march of several days the Toncahua scouts reported that they were in the immediate vicinity of the Comanche encampment. The Comanches, though proverbial for their sleepless vigilance, were unsuspicious of danger ; and so unsuspected was the approach of the rangers, that on the day preceding the battle, Col. Ford and Capt. Ross stood in the old road from Fort Smith to Santa Fe, just north of the Rio Negro or "False Wichita," and watched through their glasses the Comanches running buffalo in the valleys still more to the north. That night the Toncahua spies completed the hazardous mission of locating definitely the position of the enemy's encampment. The next morning (May 12) the rangers and "reserve" or friendly Indians, marched before sunrise to the attack.

Placido claimed for his "red warriors" the privilege of wreaking vengeance upon their hereditary enemies. His request was granted,—and the Toncahuas effected a complete surprise. The struggle was short, sharp and sanguinary. The women and children were made prisoners, but not a Comanche brave surrendered. Their savage pride preferred death to the restraints and humiliations of captivity. Not a single warrior escaped to bear the sorrowful tidings of this destructive engagement to their people.

A short time after the sun had lighted the tops of the hills, the rangers came in full view of the hostile camp, pitched in one of the picturesque valleys of the Canadian, and on the opposite side of the stream, in the immediate vicinity of the famous "Antelope Hills."

The panorama thus presented to the view of the rangers was beautiful in the extreme, and their pent-up enthusiasm found vent in a shout of exultation, which was speedily suppressed by Col. Ford. Just at this moment a solitary Comanche was descried riding southward, evidently heading for the village which Placido had so recently destroyed. He was wholly unconcious of the proximity of an enemy. Instant pursuit was now made; he turned, and fled at full speed toward the main camp across the Canadian, closely followed by the rangers. He dashed across the stream, and thus revealed to his pursuers the locality of a safe ford across the miry and almost impassable river. He rushed into the village beyond, sounding the notes of alarm; and soon the Comanche warriors presented a bold front of battle-line between their women and children and the advancing rangers. After a few minutes occupied in forming line of battle, both sides were arrayed in full force and effect. The friendly Indians were placed on the right, and thrown a little forward. Col. Ford's object was to deceive the Comanches as to the character of the attacking force, and as to the quality of arms they possessed.

Pohebits Quasho, arrayed in all the trappings of his "war toggery"—coat of mail, shield, bow and lance, completed by a head-dress decorated with feathers and long red flannel streamers; and besmeared in "war-paint,"—gaily dashed about on his "war-horse" midway of the opposing lines, delivering taunts and challenges to the whites. As the old chief dashed to and fro a number of rifles were discharged at him in point blank range without any effect whatever; which seeming immunity to death encouraged his warriors greatly; and induced even some of the more superstitious among the rangers to enquire within themselves if it were possible that "Old Iron Jacket" really bore a charmed life? Followed by a few of his braves, he

now bore down upon the rangers, described a few
"charmed circles," gave a few necromantic puffs with
his breath and let fly several arrows at Col. Ford, Capt.
Ross and chief Placido; receiving their fire without
harm. But as he approached the line of the Toncahuas, a rifle directed by the steady nerve and unerring
eye of one of their number, Jim Pockmark, brought
the "Big Medicine" to the dust. The shot was a
mortal one. The fallen chieftain was instantly surrounded by his braves, but the spirit of the conjuring
brave had taken its flight to the "happy hunting
grounds."

These incidents occupied but a brief space of time,
when the order to charge was given; and then ensued
one of the grandest assaults ever made against the
Comanches. The enthusiastic shouts of the rangers
and the triumphant yell of their red allys greeted the
welcome order. It was responded to by the defiant
"war-hoop" of the Comanches, and in those virgin
hills, remote from civilization, the saturnalia of battle
was inaugurated. The shouts of enraged combatants,
the wail of women, the piteous cries of terrified children, the howling of frightened dogs, the deadly re-
ports of rifle and revolver, constituted a discordant
confusion of sounds, blent together in an unearthly
mass of infernal noise.

The conflict was sharp and quick—a charge; a mo-
mentary exchange of rifle and arrow shots, and the

heart-rending wail of discomfiture and dismay, and the beaten Comanches abandoned their lodges and camp to the victors, and began a disorderly retreat. But sufficient method was observed to take advantage of each grove of timber, each hill and ravine, to make a stand against their pursuers; and thus enable the women and children to make their escape. The noise of battle now diverged from a common center like the spokes of a wheel, and continued to greet the ear for several hours, gradually growing fainter as the pursuit disappeared in the distance.

But another division, under the vigilant Peta Nocona, was soon marching through the hills north of the Canadian, to the rescue. Though ten miles distant, his quick ear had caught the first sounds of the battle; and soon he was riding, with Cynthia Ann by his side, at the head of (500) five hundred warriors.

About 1 o'clock of the afternoon the last of the rangers returned from the pursuit of Pohebits Quasho's discomfited braves, just in time to anticipate this threatened attack.

As Capt. Ross (who was one of the last to return) rode up, he enquired "What hour of the morning is it, Colonel?" "Morning!" exclaimed Col. Ford, "it is one o'clock of the afternoon;" so unconscious is one of the flight of time during an engagement, that the work of hours seems comprised within the space of a few moments.

"Hello! what are you in line of battle for?" asked Ross. "Look at the hills there, and you will see," calmly replied Col. Ford, pointing to the hills some half a mile distant, behind which the forces of Peta Nocona were visible; an imposing line of 500 warriors drawn up in battle array.

Col. Ford had with 221 men fought and routed over 400 Comanches, and now he was confronted by a stronger force, fresh from their village still higher up on the Canadian. They had come to drive the "pale faces" and their hated copper-colored allies from the captured camp, to retake prisoners, to retake over four hundred head of horses and an immense quantity of plunder. They did not fancy the defiant state of preparations awaiting them in the valley, however, and were waiting to avail themselves of some incautious movement on the part of the rangers, when the wily Peta Nocona with his forces would spring like a lion from his lair, and with one combined and desperate effort swoop down and annihilate the enemy. But his antagonist was a soldier of too much sagacity to allow any advantage to a vigilant foe.

The two forces remained thus contemplating each other for over an hour; during which time a series of operations ensued between single combatants illustrat-

ive of the Indian mode of warfare, and the marked
difference between the nomadic Comanche and his
semi-civilized congeners, the Tonchua. The Ton-
chuas took advantage of ravines, trees and other natural shelter. Their arms were rifles and "six-shooters."
The Comanches came to the attack with shield and
bow and lance, mounted on gaily caparisoned and
prancing steeds, and flaunting feathers and all the
"georgeous" display incident to savage "finery" and
pomp. They are probably the most expert equestri-
ans in the world. A Comanche warrior would gaily
canter to a point half way between the opposing lines,
yell a defiant "war hoop," and shake his shield. This
was a challenge to single combat.

Several of the friendly Indians who accepted such
challenges were placed *hors de combat* by their more
expert adversaries, and in consequence Col. Ford ordered them to decline the savage banters; much to the
dissatisfaction of Placido, who had conducted himself
throughout the series of engagements with the bearing
of a savage hero.

Says Col. Ford: "In these combats the mind of the
spectator was vividly carried back to the days of chiv-
alry; the jousts and tournaments of knights; and to
the concomitants of those scenic exhibitions of gallantry. The feats of horsemanship were splendid, the
lances and shields were used with great dexterity, and

the whole performance was a novel show to civilized man."

Col. Ford now ordered Placido, with a part of his warriors, to advance in the direction of the enemy, and if possible draw them in the valley, so as to afford the rangers an opportunity to charge them. This had the desired effect, and the rangers were ready to deliver a charge, when it was discovered that the friendly Indians had removed the white badges from their heads because they served as targets for the Comanches, consequently the rangers were unable to distinguish friend from foe. This necessitated the entire withdrawal of the Indians. The Comanches witnessed these preparations and now commenced to recoil. The rangers advanced; the trot, the gallop, the headlong charge, followed in rapid succession. Lieut. Nelson made a skillful movement and struck the enemy's left flank. The Comanche line was broken. A running fight for three or four miles ensued. The enemy was driven back wherever he made a stand. The most determined resistance was made in a timbered ravine. Here one of Placido's warriors was killed, and one of the rangers, young George W. Pascal wounded. The Comanches left some dead upon the spot and had several more wounded. After routing them at this point the rangers continued to pursue them some distance, intent upon taking the women and children prisoners; but Peta

Nocona, by the exercise of those commanding qualities which had often before signalized his conduct on the field, succeeded in covering their retreat, and thus allowing them to escape. It was now about 4 P. M., both horses and men were almost entirely exhausted, and Col. Ford ordered a halt and returned to the village.

Brave old Placido and his warriors fought like so many demons. It was difficult to restrain them, so anxious were they to wreak vengeance on the Comanches.

In all of these engagements seventy-five (75) Comanches "bit the dust."

The loss of the rangers was small,—two killed and five or six wounded.

The trophies of Pohebits Quasho, including his lance, bow, shield, head-dress and the celebrated coat of scale mail, was deposited by Col. Ford in the State archives at Austin, where, doubtless, they may yet be seen,—as curious relics of by-gone days.

The lamented old chief, Placido, fell a victim to the revengeful Comanches during the latter part of the great civil war, between the North and South; being assassinated by a party of his enemies on the reservation, near Fort Sill.

The venerable John Henry Brown, some years since, paid a merited tribute to his memory through the columns of the Dallas *Herald*.

Of Placido it has been said that he was the "soul of honor," and "never betrayed a trust." That he was brave to the utmost, we have only to refer to his numerous exploits during his long and gratuitous service on our frontiers. He was implicitly trusted by Burleson and other partisan leaders; and rendered invaluable services in behalf of the early Texian pioneers; in recognition of which he never recieved any reward of a material nature, beyond a few paltry pounds of gun-powder and salt. Imperial Texas should rear a monument commemorative of his memory. He was the more than Tammany of Texas! But I am digressing from the narrative proper.

"Doubtless," says Rose, "Cynthia Ann rode from this ill-starred field with her infant daughter pressed to her bosom, and her sons—two youths of about ten and twelve years of age, at her side,—as fearful of capture at the hands of the hated whites, as years ago—immediately after the massacre of Parker's Fort—she had been anxious for the same."

GENERAL L S ROSS.

CHAPTER IV.

Genl. L. S. Ross.—Battle of the Wichita.

It is not our purpose in this connection, to assume the role of biographer to so distinguished a personage as is the chevalier Bayard of Texas—General Lawrence Sullivan Ross. That task should be left to an abler pen; and besides, it would be impossible to do anything like justice to the romantic, adventurous, and altogether splendid and brilliant career of the brave and daring young ranger who rescued Cynthia Ann Parker from captivity, at least in the circumscribed limits of a brief biographical sketch, such as we shall be compelled to confine ourself to; yet, some brief mention of his services and exploits as a ranger captain, by way of an introduction to the reader beyond the limits of Texas, where his name and fame are as household words, is deemed necessary, hence we beg leave here to give a brief sketch of his life.

"Texas, though her annals be brief," says the author of "Ross' Texas Brigade," counts upon her "roll of honor" the names of many heros, living and dead. Their splendid services are the inestimable legacies of the past and present, to the future. Of the latter, it is the high prerogative of the State to enbalm their names and memories as perpetual examples to excite the generous emulation of the Texian youth to the latest posterity. Of the former it is our pleasant province to accord them those honors which their services, in so eminent a degree, entitle them to receive. Few lands, since the days of the "Scottish Chiefs," have furnished material upon which to predicate a Douglas, a Wallace, or a Ravenswood; and the adventures of chivalric enterprise, arrant quest of danger, and the personal combat, were relegated, together with the knight's armorial trappings, to the rusty archives of "Tower" and "Pantheon," until the Comanche Bedouins of the Texian plains tendered in bold defiance the savage gauntlet to the pioneer knights of progress and civilization. And though her heraldic roll glows with the names of a Houston, a Rusk, Lamar, McCulloch, Hayes, Chevellie, which illumine the pages of her history with an effulgence of glory, Texas never nurtured on her maternal bosom a son of more filial devotion, of more loyal patriotism, or indomitable will to do and dare, than L. S. Ross."

Lawrence Sullivan Ross was born in the village of Bentonsport, Ohio, in the year 1838. His father, Captain S. P. Ross, emigrated to Texas in 1839, casting his fortunes with the struggling pioneers who were blazing the pathway of civilization into the wilds of a *terra incognita*, as Texas then was.

"Captain S. P. Ross was, for many years, pre-eminent as a leader against the implacable savages, who made frequent incursions into the settlements. The duty of repelling these forays usually devolved upon Captain Ross and his neighbors, and, for many years, his company constituted the only bulwark of safety between the feeble colonist and the scalping knife. The rapacity and treachery of his Comanche and Kiowa foes demanded of Captain Ross sleepless vigilance, acute sagacity, and a will that brooked no obstacle or danger. It was in the performance of this arduous duty that he slew, in single combat, "Big Foot," a Comanche chief of great prowess, and who was for many years the scourge of the early Texas frontier. The services of Captain S. P. Ross are still held in grateful remembrance by the descendants of his compatriots, and his memory will never be suffered to pass away while Texians feel a pride in the sterling worth of the pioneers who laid the foundation of Texas' greatness and glory.— *Vide* *"Ross' Texas Brigade,"* p. 158.

The following incident, as illustrative of the character and spirit of the man and times, is given: "On one occasion, Captain Ross, who had been visiting a neighbor, was returning home, afoot, accompanied by his little son, 'Sul,' as the General was familiarly called. When within half a mile of his house, he was

surrounded by fifteen or twenty mounted Comanche
warriors, who commenced an immediate attack. The
Captain, athletic and swift of foot, threw his son on
his back, and outran their ponies to the house, escap-
ing unhurt amid a perfect shower of arrows.''

Such were among the daily experiences of the child,
and with such impressions stamped upon the infantile
mind, it was but natural that the enthusiastic spirit of
the ardent youth should lead him to such adventures
upon the ''war-path,'' similar to those that had signalized his honored father's prowess upon so many occasions.

Hence, we find ''Sul'' Ross, during vacation from
his studies at Florence Weslean University, Alabama,
though a beardless boy, scarcely twenty years of age,
in command of a contingent of 135 friendly Indians,
co-operating with the United States cavalry under the
dashing Major Earl Van Dorn, in a compaign against
the Comanches.

*   *   *   *   *   *   *   *

Notwithstanding the severe chastisement that had
been inflicted on the Comanches at ''Antelope Hills,''
they soon renewed their hostilities, committing many
depredations and murders during the summer of 1858.

Early in September Major Van Dorn received orders from Gen. Twiggs, to equip four companies, including Ross' ''red warriors,'' and go out on a scout-

ing expedition against the hostile Indians. This he did, penetrating the heart of the Indian country where he proceeded to build a stockade, placing within it all the pack mules, extra horses and supplies, which was left in charge of the infantry.

Ross' faithful Indian scouts soon reported the discovery of a large Comanche village near the Wichita Mountains, about ninety miles away. The four companies, attended by the spies, immediately set out for the village, and after a fatiguing march of thirty-six hours, causing the men to be continuously in the saddle the latter sixteen hours of the ride, arrived in the immediate vicinity of the Indian camp just at daylight on the morning of October 1st.

A reconnoissance showed that the wily Comanches were not apprehensive of an attack, and were sleeping in fancied security. The horses of the tribe, which consisted of a *caballado* of about 500 head, were grazing near the outskirts of the village. Major Van Dorn directed Captain Ross, at the head of his Indians, to "round up" the horses, and drive them from the camp, which was effected speedily, and thus the Comanches were forced to fight on foot—a proceeding extremely harrowing to the proud warriors' feelings.

"Just as the sun was peeping above the eastern horizon," says Victor M. Rose, whose graphic narrative we again quote, "Van Dorn charged the upper

end of the village, while Ross' command, in conjunc-
tion with a detachment of United States cavalry,
charged the lower. The village was strung out along
the banks of a branch for several hundred yards. The
morning was very foggy, and after a few moments of
firing the smoke and fog became so dense that objects
at but a short distance could be distinguished only with
great difficulty. The Comanches fought with absolute
desperation, and contended for every advantage, as
their women and children, and all their possessions,
were in peril.

"A few moments after the engagement became general, Ross discovered a number of Comanches running
down to the branch, about one hundred and fifty yards
from the village, and concluded that they were beating
a retreat. Immediately, Ross, Lieutenant Van Camp
of the United States Army, Alexander, a 'regular'
soldier, and one Caddo Indian, of Ross' command,
ran to the point with the intention of intercepting them.
Arriving, it was discovered that the fugitives were the
women and children. In a moment, another posse of
women and children came running immediately past
the squad of Ross, who, discovering a little white girl
among the number, made his Caddo Indian grab her
as she was passing. The little pale-face—apparently
about twelve years of age—was badly frightened at
finding herself a captive to a strange Indian and

stranger white men, and was hard to manage at first.
"Ross now discovered, through the fog and smoke
of the battle, that a band of some twenty-five Comanche warriors had cut his small party off from com-
munication with Van Dorn, and were bearing immediately down upon them. They shot Lieutenant Van
Camp through the heart, killing him ere he could fire
his double-barrelled shot-gun. ., Alexander, the United
States Cavalryman, was likewise shot down before he
could fire his gun (a rifle). Ross was armed with a
Sharp's rifle, and attempted to fire upon the exultant
red devils, but the cap snapped. 'Mohee,' a Comanche warrior, siezed Alexander's rifle and shot Ross
down. The indomitable young ranger fell upon the
side on which his pistol was borne, and though partially
paralyzed by the shot, he turned himself, and was get-
ting his pistol out when 'Mohee' drew his butcher-
knife, and started towards his prostrate foe—some
fifteen feet away—with the evident design of stabbing
and scalping him. He made but a few steps, however,
when one of his companions cried out something in the
Comanche tongue, which was a signal to the band,
and they broke away in confusion. 'Mohee' ran
about twenty steps, when a wire-cartridge, containing
nine buck-shot, fired from a gun in the hands of Lieutenant James Majors, (afterwards a Confederate General), struck him between the shoulders, and he fell

forward on his face, dead. 'Mohee' was an old acquaintance of Ross, as the latter had seen him frequently at his father's post on the frontier, and recognized him as soon as their eyes met. The faithful Caddo held on to the little girl throughout this desperate *melee*, and, strange to relate, neither were harmed. The Caddo, doubtless, owed his escape to the fact that the Comanches were fearful of wounding or killing the little girl. This whole scene transpired in a few moments, and Captain N. G. Evans' company of the Second United States Cavalry, had taken possession of the lower end of the Comanche village, and Major Van Dorn held the upper, and the Comanches were running into the hills and brush; not, however, before an infuriated Comanche shot the gallant Van Dorn with an arrow. Van Dorn fell, and it was supposed that he was mortally wounded. In consequence of their wounds, the two chieftains were compelled to remain on the battle ground five or six days. After the expiration of this time, Ross' Indians made a 'litter,' after their fashion, borne between two gentle mules, and in it placed their heroic and beloved 'boy captain,' and set out for the settlements at Fort Belknap. When this mode of conveyance would become too painful, by reason of the rough, broken nature of the country, these brave Caddos—whose race and history are but synonyms of courage and fidelity—would vie with each other in bearing the burden upon their own shoulders. At Camp Radziminski, occupied by United States forces, an ambulance was obtained, and the remainder of the journey made with comparative comfort. Major Van Dorn was also conveyed to Radziminski. He speedily recovered of his wound, and soon made another brilliant campaign against the Comanches, as we shall see further on. Ross recovered sufficiently in a few weeks so as to be able to return to college at Florence, Alabama, where he completed his studies, and graduated in 1859."

This was the battle of the Wichita Mountains, a hotly contested and most desperate hand to hand fight in which the two gallant and dashing young officers, Ross and Van Dorn, were severely wounded. The loss of the whites was five killed and several wounded.

The loss of the Comanches was, eighty or ninety warriors killed, many wounded, and several captured; besides losing all their horses, camp equipage, supplies, etc.

The return of this victorious little army was hailed with enthusiastic rejoicing and congratulation, and the Wichita fight and Van Dorn and Ross were the themes of song and story for many years along the borders and in the halls and banqueting-rooms of the cities, and the martial music of the "Wichita March" resounded through the plains of Texas wherever the Second

Cavalry encamped or rode off on scouts in after years.

The little girl captive—of whose parentage or history nothing could be ascertained, though strenuous efforts were made—was christened "Lizzie Ross," in honor of Miss *Lizzie* Tinsley, daughter of Dr. D. R. Tinsley, of Waco, to whom Ross at that time was engaged; and afterwards married—May, 1861.

Of Lizzie Ross, it can be said that, in her career, is afforded a thorough verification of Lord Byron's saying: "Truth is stranger than fiction!" She was adopted by her brave and generous captor, properly reared and educated, and became a beautiful and accomplished woman. Here were sufficient romance and vicissitude, in the brief career of a little maiden, to have turned the "roundelay's" of "troubadour and meunesauger." A solitary lily, blooming amidst the wildest grasses of the desert plains. A little Indian girl in all save the Caucasian's conscious stamp of superiority. Torn from home, perhaps, amid the heart-rending scenes of rapine, torture and death. A stranger to race and lineage—stranger even to the tongue in which a mother's lullaby was breathed. Affiliating with these wild Ishmaelites of the prairie—a Comanche in all things save the intuitive premonition *that she was not of them!* Finally, redeemed from a captivity worse than death by a knight entitled to rank, for all

LIZZIE ROSS.

time in the history of Texas, *"primus inter pores."*
Vide *"Ross Texas Brigade,"* p. 178.

Lizzie Ross accompanied Gen. Ross' mother on a
visit to the State of California, a few years since, and
while there, became the wife of a wealthy merchant
near Los Angeles, where she now resides.

Such is the romantic story of "Lizzie Ross"—a
story that derives additional interest because of the fact
of its absolute truth in all respects.[1]

(1.—The following letter from Gen. L. S. Ross, touching upon the
battle of the Wichita Mountains and the re-capture of "Lizzie Ross," is
here appropriately inserted:

"WACO, TEXAS, July 12. 1884.

"MR. JAMES T. DESHIELDS. *Dear Sir*:—My father could give
you reliable data enough to fill a volume. I send you photograph of
Cynthia Ann Parker, with notes relating to her on back of photo. On
the 28th of October, 1858, I had a battle with the Comanches at Wichita
Mts., and there recaptured a little white girl about eight years old,
whose parentage, nor indeed any trace of her kindred, was ever found.
I adopted, reared, and educated her, giving her the name of Lizzie Ross;
the former name being in honor of the young lady—Lizzie Tinsley—to
whom I was then engaged and afterwards married—May, 1861.

"Lizzie Ross grew to womanhood, and married a wealthy merchant
living near Los Angeles, California, where she now resides. See History
of 'Ross' Brigade' by Victor M. Rose, and published by Courier-Jour-
nal, for a full and graphic description of the battle and other notable incidents. I could give you many interesting as well as thrilling adventures of self and father's family with the Indians in the early settlement
of the country.

"He can give you more information than any living Texian, touching the Indian character, having been their agent and warm and trusted
friend, in whom they had confidence.

"My early life was one of constant danger from their forays, and I
was twice in their hands and at their mercy, as well as the other members of my father's family.

"But I am just now too busy with my farm matters to give you such
data as would subserve your purpose.

"Yours truly, L. S. ROSS."

CHAPTER V.

Battle of Pease River.—Cynthia Ann Parker.

For some time after Ross' victory at the Wichita Mountains the Comanches were less hostile, seldom penetrating far down into the settlements. But in 1859–'60 the condition of the frontier was again truly deplorable. The people were obliged to stand in a continued posture of defense, and were in continual alarm and hazard of their lives, never daring to stir abroad unarmed, for small bodies of savages, quick-sighted and accustomed to perpetual watchfulness, hovered on the outskirts, and springing from behind bush or rock, ·surprised his enemy before he was aware of danger, and sent tidings of his presence in the fatal blow, and after execution of the bloody work, by superior knowledge of the country and rapid movements, safely retired to their inaccessable deserts.

In the Autumn of 1860 the indomitable and fearless Peta Nocona led a raiding party of Comanches through Parker county, so named in honor of the family of his wife, Cynthia Ann, committing great depredations as they passed through. The venerable Isaac Parker was at the time a resident of the town of Weatherford, the county seat; and little did he imagine that the chief of the ruthless savages who spread desolation and death on every side as far as their arms could reach, was the husband of his long lost niece; and that the comingled blood of the murdered Parkers and the atrocious Comanche now coursed in the veins of a second generation—bound equally by the ties of consanguinity to murderer and murdered; that the son of Peta Nocona and Cynthia Ann Parker would become the chief of the proud Comanches, whose boast it is that their constitutional settlement of government is the purest democracy ever originated and administered among men. It certainly conserved the object of its institution—the protection and happiness of the people—for a longer period, and much more satisfactorily than has that of any other Indian tribe. The Comanches claimed a superiority over the other Texian tribes; and they unquestionably were more intelligent and courageous. The "Reservation Policy,"—necessary though it be—brings them all to an object level, —the plane of lazy beggars and thieves. The Comanche is the most qualified by nature for receiving education and for adapting himself to the requirements of civilization, of all the southern tribes, not excepting even the Cherokees, with their churches, school-houses and farms. The Comanches after waging an unceasing war for nearly fifty years against the United States, Texas and Mexico, still number 16,000 souls; a far better showing than any other tribe can make, though

not one but has enjoyed privileges to which the Comanche was a stranger. It is a shame to the civilization of the age that a people so susceptible of a high
degree of development should be allowed to grovel in
the depths of heathenism and savagery. But we are
digressing.

The loud and clamorous cries of the settlers along
the frontier for protection, induced the Government to
organize and send out a regiment under Col. M. T.
Johnson to take the field for public defense. But these
efforts proved of small service. The expedition,
though at great expense to the state, failed to find an
Indian until returning, the command was followed by
the wily Comanches, their horses "stampeded" at
night and most of the men compelled to reach the settlements on foot, under great suffering and exposure.

Captain "Sul" Ross, who had just graduated from
Florence Wesleyan University, of Alabama, and returned to Texas, was commissioned a captain of rangers, by Governor Sam Houston, and directed to organize a company of sixty men, with orders to repair to
Fort Belknap, receive from Col. Johnson all government property, as his regiment was disbanded, and
take the field against the redoubtable Peta Nocona, and
afford the frontier such protection as was possible to
this small force. The necessity of vigorous measures
soon became so pressing that Capt. Ross determined to

attempt to curb the insolence of these implacable enemies of Texas by following them into their fastnesses and carry the war into their own homes. In his graphic narration of this campaign Gen. L. S. Ross says: "As I could take but forty of my men from my post, I requested Capt. N. G. Evans, in command of the United States troops, at Camp Cooper, to send me a detachment of the Second Cavalry. We had been intimately connected on the Van Dorn campaign, during which I was the recipient of much kindness from Capt. Evans while I was suffering from a severe wound received from an Indian in the battle of the 'Wichita.' He promptly sent me a sergeant and twenty well mounted men. My force was still further augmented by some seventy volunteer citizens under command of the brave old frontiersman, Capt. Jack Cureton, of Bosque county. These self-sacrificing patriots, without the hope of pay or reward, left their de-defenseless homes and families to avenge the sufferings of the frontier people. With pack-mules laden down with necessary supplies the expedition marched for the Indian country.

"On the 18th of December, 1860, while marching up Pease river, I had some suspicions that Indians were in the vicinity, by reason of the buffalo that came running in great numbers from the north towards us, and while my command moved in the low ground I visited all neighboring high points to make discoveries. On one of these sand hills I found four fresh pony tracks, and being satisfied that Indian videtts had just gone, I galloped forward about a mile to a higher point, and riding to the top, to my inexpressable surprise, found myself within 200 yards of a Comanche village, located on a small stream winding around the base of the hill. It was a most happy circumstance that a piercing north wind was blowing, bearing with it clouds of sand, and my presence was unobserved and the surprise complete. By signaling my men as I stood concealed, they reached me without being discovered by the Indians, who were busy packing up preparatory to a move. By this time the Indians mounted and moved off north across the level plain. My command, with the detachment of the Second Cavalry, had out-marched and become separated from the citizen command, which left me about sixty men. In making disposition for attack, the sergeant and his twenty men were sent at a gallop, behind a chain of sand hills, to encompass them in and cut off their retreat, while with forty men I charged. The attack was so sudden that a considerable number were killed before they could prepare for defense. They fled precipitately right into the presence of the sergeant and his men. Here they met with a warm reception, and finding themselves completely encompassed, every one fled his own way, and was hotly pursued and hard pressed.

"The chief of the party, Peta Nocona, a noted warrior of great repute, with a young girl about fifteen years of age mounted on his horse behind him, and Cynthia Ann Parker, with a girl child about two years of age in her arms and mounted on a fleet pony, fled together, while Lieut. Tom. Kelliheir and I pursued them. After running about a mile Killiheir ran up by the side of Cynthia's horse, and I was in the act of shooting when she held up her child and stopped. I kept on after the chief and about a half a mile further, when in about twenty yards of him I fired my pistol, striking the girl (whom I supposed to be a man, as she rode like one, and only her head was visible above the buffalo robe with which she was wrapped) near the heart, killing her instantly, and the same ball would have killed both but for the shield of the chief, which hung down, covering his back. When the girl fell from the horse she pulled him off also, but he caught on his feet, and before steadying himself, my horse, running at full speed, was very nearly upon top of him, when he was struck with an arrow, which caused him to fall to pitching or 'bucking,' and it was with great difficulty that I kept my saddle, and in the meantime, narrowly escaped several arrows coming in quick succession from the chief's bow. Being at such

disadvantage he would have killed me in a few minutes
but for a random shot from my pistol (while I was
clinging with my left hand to the pommel of my saddle) which broke his right arm at the elbow, completely disabling him. My horse then became quiet, and I
shot the chief twice through the body, whereupon he
deliberately walked to a small tree, the only one in
sight, and leaning against it, began to sing a wild,
wierd song. At this time my Mexican servant, who
had once been a captive with the Comanches and spoke
their language as fluently as his mother tongue, came
up, in company with two of my men. I then sum-
moned the chief to surrender, but he promptly treated
every overture with contempt, and signalized this declaration with a savage attempt to thrust me with the
lance which he held in his left hand. I could only
look upon him with pity and admiration. For, deplorable as was his situation, with no chance of escape,
his party utterly destroyed, his wife and child captured
in his sight, he was undaunted by the fate that awaited
him, and as he seemed to prefer death to life, I directed the Mexican to end his misery by a charge of buck-
shot from the gun which he carried. Taking up his
accouterments, which I subsequently sent Gov. Houston, to be deposited in the archives at Austin, we rode
back to Cynthia Ann and Killiheir, and found him bit-
terly cursing himself for having run his pet horse so

hard after an 'old squaw.' She was very dirty, both in her scanty garments and her person. But as soon as I looked on her face, I said, 'Why, Tom, this is a white woman, Indians do not have blue eyes.' On the way to the village, where my men were assembling with the spoils, and a large *caballado* of 'Indian ponies,' I discovered an Indian boy about nine years of age, secreted in the grass. Expecting to be killed, he began crying, but I made him mount behind me, and carried him along. And when in after years I frequently proposed to send him to his people, he steadfastly refused to go, and died in McLennan county last year.

"After camping for the night Cynthia Ann kept crying, and thinking it was caused from fear of death at our hands, I had the Mexican tell her that we recognized her as one of our own people, and would not harm her. She said two of her boys were with her when the fight began, and she was distressed by the fear that they had been killed. It so happened, however, both escaped, and one of them, 'Quanah' is now a chief. The other died some years ago on the plains. I then asked her to give me the history of her life with the Indians, and the circumstances attending her capture by them, which she promptly did in a very sensible manner. And as the facts detailed corresponded with the massacre at Parker's Fort, I was impressed with the belief that she was Cynthia Ann Parker. Returning to my post, I sent her and child to the ladies at Cooper, where she could recieve the attention her situation demanded, and at the same time dispatched a messenger to Col. Parker, her uncle, near Weatherford, and as I was called to Waco to meet Gov. Houston, I left directions for the Mexican to accompany Col. Parker to Cooper in the capacity of interpreter. When he reached there, her identity was soon discovered to Col. Parker's entire satisfaction and great happiness."

And thus was fought the battle of "Pease river" between a superior force of Comanches under the implacable chief, Peta Nocona on one side, and sixty rangers led by their youthful commander, Capt. L. S. Ross, on the other. Ross, sword in hand, led the furious rush of the rangers; and in the desperate encounter of "war to the knife" which ensued, nearly all the warriors bit the dust.

So signal a victory had never before been gained over the fierce and war-like Comanches; and never since that fatal December day in 1860 have they made any military demonstrations at all commensurate with the fame of their proud campaigns in the past. The great Comanche confederacy was forever broken. The incessant and sanguinary war which had been waged for more than thirty years was now virtually at an end.

The blow was a most decisive one ; as sudden and irresistible as a thunder-bolt, and as remorseless and crushing as the hand of Fate.

It was a short but desperate conflict. Victory trembled in the balance. A determined charge, accompanied by a simultaneous fire from the solid phalanx of yelling rangers and the Comanches beat a hasty retreat, leaving many dead and wounded upon the field. Espying the chief and a chosen few riding at full speed, and in a different direction from the other fugitives, from the ill-starred field, Ross quickly pursued. Divining his purpose, the watchful Peta Nocona rode at full speed, but was soon overtaken, when the two chiefs engaged in a personal encounter, which must result in the death of one or the other. Peta Nocona fell, and his last sigh was taken up in mournful wailings on the wings of defeat. Most of the women and children with a few warriors escaped. Many of these perished on the cold and inhospitable plains, in an effort to reach their friends on the head-waters of the Arkansas river.

The immediate fruits of the victory was some four hundred and fifty horses, and their accumulated winter's supply of food. But the incidental fruits are not to be computed on the basis of dollars and cents. The proud spirit of the Comanche was here broken, and to this signal defeat is to be attributed the measurably pacific conduct of these heretofore implacable foes of the white race during the course of the late civil war in the Union,—a boon of incalculable value to Texas.

In a letter recognizing the great service rendered the state by Ross in dealing the Comanches this crushing blow, Governor Houston said:

"Your success in protecting the frontier gives me great satisfaction. I am satisfied that with the same opportunities, you would rival, if not excel, the greatest exploits of McCulloch and Hays. Continue to repel, pursue, and punish every body of Indians coming into the State, and the people will not withhold their praise."   Signed: SAM HOUSTON.

QUANAH PARKER.

CHAPTER VI.

Cynthia Ann Parker.—Quanah Parker.

From May 19th, 1836, to December 18th, 1860, was twenty-four years and seven months. Add to this nine years, her age when captured, and at the later date Cynthia Ann Parker was in her thirty-fourth year. During the last ten years of this quarter of a century, which she spent as a captive among the Comanches, no tidings had been received of her. She had long been given up as dead or irretrievably lost to civilization.

Notwithstanding the long lapse of time which had intervened since the Capture of Cynthia Ann Parker, Ross, as he interrogated his "blue eyed" but bronzed captive, more than suspected that she was the veritable "Cynthia Ann Parker," of which he had heard so much from his boyhood. She was dressed in female attire, of course, according to the custom of the Comanches, which being very similar to that of the males, doubtless, gave rise to the eroneous statement that she was dressed in male costume. So sure was Ross of her identity that, as before stated, he at once dispatched a messenger to her uncle, the venerable Isaac Parker; in the meantime placing Cynthia Ann in charge of Mrs.

Evans, wife of Capt. N. G. Evans, the commandant at Fort Cooper, who at once, with commendable benevolence, administered to her necessities.

Upon the arrival of Col. Parker at Fort Cooper, interrogations were made her through the Mexican interpreter, for she remembered not one word of English, respecting her identity; but she had forgotten absolutely everything, apparently, at all connected with her family or past history.

In dispair of being able to reach a conclusion, Col. Parker was about to leave, when he said, "The name of my niece was Cynthia Ann." The sound of the once familiar name, doubtless the last lingering memento of the old home at the fort, seemed to touch a responsive chord in her nature, when a sign of intelligence lighted up her countenance, as memory by some mystic inspiration resumed its cunning as she looked up, and patting her breast, said, "Cynthia Ann! Cynthia Ann!" At the awakening of this single spark of reminiscence, the sole gleam in the mental gloom of many years, her countenance brightened with a pleasant smile in place of the sullen expression which habitually characterizes the looks of an Indian restrained of freedom. There was now no longer any doubt as to her identity with the little girl lost and mourned so long. It was in reality Cynthia Ann Parker,—but, O, so changed!

But as savage-like and dark of complexion as she was, Cynthia Ann was still dear to her overjoyed uncle, and was welcomed home by relatives with all the joyous transports with which the prodigal son was hailed upon his miserable return to the parental roof.

As thorough an Indian in manner and looks as if she had been so born, she sought every opportunity to escape, and had to be closely watched for some time. Her uncle carried herself and child to his home, then took them to Austin, where the secession convention was in session. Mrs. John Henry Brown and Mrs. N. C. Raymond interested themselves in her, dressed her neatly, and on one occasion took her into the gallery of the hall while the convention was in session. They soon realized that she was greatly alarmed by the belief that the assemblage was a council of chiefs, sitting in judgment on her life. Mrs. Brown beckoned to her husband, Hon. John Henry Brown, who was a member of the convention, who appeared and succeeded in reassuring her that she was among friends.

Gradually her mother tongue came back, and with it occasional incidents of her childhood, including a recognition of the venerable Mr. Anglin, and perhaps one or two others.

The civil war coming on soon after, which necessitated the resumption of such primitive arts, she learned to spin, weave and to perform the domestic duties.

She proved quite an adept in such work, and became a very useful member of the household.

The ruling passion of her bosom seemed to be the maternal instinct, and she cherished the hope that when the war was concluded she would at last succeed in re-claiming her two children who were still with the Indians. But it was written otherwise, and Cynthia Ann and her little "barbarian" were called hence ere "the cruel war was over." She died at her brother's in Anderson county, Texas, in 1864, preceded a short time by her sprightly little daughter, "Prairie Flower."

Thus ended the sad story of a woman far famed along the border.

*   *   *   *   *   *   *   *

How fared it with the two young orphans we may only imagine. The lot of these helpless ones is too often one of trials, heart-pangs, and want, even among our enlightened people; and it would require a painful recital to follow the children of Peta Nocona and Cynthia Ann Parker from the terrible fight on Pease river, across trackless prairies, and rugged mountain-ways, in the inhospitable month of December, tired, hungry, and carrying a load upon their hearts far heavier than the physical evils which so harshly beset them. Their father was slain, and their mother a captive. Doubtless they were as intent upon her future recovery, during the many years in which they shared the vicissitudes of their people, until the announcement of her death reached them, as her own family had been for her rescue during her quarter of a century of captivity. One of the little sons of Cynthia Ann died some years after her recapture. The other, now known as Capt. Quanah Parker, born as he says in 1854, is the chief of Comanches, on their reservation in the Indian Territory.   Bancroft Library

Finally, in 1874, the Comanches were forced upon a "reservation," near Fort Sill, to lead the beggarly life of "hooded harlots and blanketed thieves," and it was at this place that the "war-chief" Quanah, learned that it was possible he might secure a photograph of his mother.[1]

An advertisement to that effect was inserted in the Fort Worth *Gazette*, when General Ross at once forwarded him a copy. To his untutored mind it seemed that a miracle had been wrought in response to his "paper prayer;" and his exclamations, as he gazed intently and long upon the faithful representation of "Preloch," or Cynthia Ann, were highly suggestive of Cowper's lines on his mother's picture; and we take

(1—Mr. A. F. Corning was at Fort Worth in 1862, when Cynthia Ann Parker passed through there. He (Mr. C.) prevailed on her to go with him to a daguerreotype gallery (there were no photographs then) and have her picture taken. Mr. Corning still has this daguerreotype, and says it is an excellent likeness of the woman as she looked then. It is now at the Academy of Art, Waco, and several photographs have been taken from it, one of which was sent to Quanah Parker, and another to the writer, from which the frontispiece to this work was engraved.

the liberty of briefly presenting a portion of the same in verse :

My mother! and do my weeping eyes once more—
Half doubting—scan thy cherished features o'er?
Yes, 'tis the pictured likeness of my dead mother,
How true to life!   It seems to breathe and move ;
Fire, love, and sweetness o'er each feature melt ;
The face expresses all the spirit felt ;
Here, while I gaze within those large, dark eyes,
I almost see the living spirit rise ;
While lights and shadows, all harmonious, glow,
And heavenly radiance settles on that brow.
What is the "medicine" I must not know,
Which thus can give to death life's bloom and glow.
O, could the white man's magic art but give
As well the happy power, and bid her live!
My name, me thinks, would be the first to break
The seal of silence, on those lips, and wake
Once more the smile that charmed her gentle face,
As she was wont to fold me in her warm embrace.
Yes, it is she, "Preloch," Nocona's pale-faced bride,
Who rode, a matchless princess, at his side,
'Neath many a bloody moon afar,
O'er tortuous paths devoted alone to war.
Long since she's joined him on that blissful shore,—
Where parting and heart-breakings are no more,—
And since our star with *him* went down in gloom,
No more to shine above the blighting doom,
'Neath which my people's hopes, alas, are fled,
I, too, but long that silent path to tread,—
A child, to be with her and him again,
Healed every wound an orphan's heart can pain !

Quanah Parker is a Nocone, which means wanderer, but on the capture of his mother, Preloch, and death of his father, Quanah was adopted and cared for by the Cohoites, and when just arrived at manhood, was made chief by his benefactors on account of his bravery. His name before he became a chief was Cepe. He has lived among several tribes of the Comanches. He was at one time with the Cochetaker, or Buffalo Eaters, and was the most influential chief of the Penatakers. Quanah is at present one of the four chiefs of the Cohoites, who each have as many people as he has. The Cohoite Comanches were never on a reservation until 1874, but are to-day further advanced in civilization than any Indians on the "Comanche reservation." Quanah speaks English, is considerably advanced in civilization, and owns a ranche with considerable live stock and a small farm; wears a citizen's suit, and conforms to the customs of civilization—withal a fine-looking and dignified son of the plains. In 1884, Quanah, in company with two other prominent Comanche chiefs, visited Mexico. In reporting their passage through that city, the San Antonio *Light* thus speaks of them:

"They bear relationship to each other of chief and two subordinates. Quanah Parker is the chief, and as he speaks very good English, they will visit the City of Mexico before they return. They came from Kiowa, Comanche and Wichita Indian Agency, and Parker bears a paper from Indian Agent Hunt that he, Parker, is a son of Cynthia Ann Parker, and is one of the most prominent chiefs of the half-breed Comanche tribe. He is also a successful stock man and farmer. He wears a citizen's suit of black, neatly fitting, regular "tooth-pick" dude shoes, a watch and gold chain and black felt hat. The only peculiar item in his appearance is his long hair, which he wears in two plaits down his back. His two braves also wear civilization's garb. But wear heavy boots, into which their trousers are thrust in true western fashion. They speak nothing but their native language."

In 1885 Quanah Parker visited the World's Fair at New Orleans.

The following extract from the Fort Worth *Gazette*, is a recent incident in his career:

"HE BLEW OUT THE GAS"

And on That Breath the Soul of Yellow Bear Flew to its Happy Hunting Grounds.

Another Instance in Which the Noble Red Man Succumbs to the Influence of Civilization!

"A sensation was created on the streets yesterday by the news of a tragedy from asphyxiation at the Pickwick hotel, of which two noted Indians, Quanah Parker and Yellow Bear, were the victims.　　　*　　*　　*

"The circumstances of the unfortunate affair were very difficult to obtain because of the inability of the

only two men who were possessed of definite information on the subject to reveal it—one on account of death, and the other from unconsciousness. The Indians arrived here yesterday from the Territory, on the Fort Worth & Denver incoming train. They registered at the Pickwick and were asigned an apartment together in the second story of the building. * *
Very little is known of their subsequent movements, but from the best evidence that can be collected it appears that Yellow Bear retired alone about 10 o'clock, and that in his utter ignorance of modern appliances, he blew out the gas. Parker, it is believed, did not seek his room until 2 or 3 o'clock in the morning, when, not detecting from some cause the presence of gas in the atmosphere, or not locating its origin in the room, he shut the door and scrambled into bed, unmindful of the deadly forces which were even then operating so disastrously. * * * *

"The failure of the two Indians to appear at breakfast or dinner caused the hotel clerk to send a man around to awake them. He found the door locked and was unable to get a response from the inmates. The room was then forceably entered, and as the door swung back the rush of the deathly perfume through the aperture told the story. A gastly spectacle met the eyes of the hotel employes. By the bedside in a crouched position, with his face pressed to the floor, was Yellow

Bear, in the half-nude condition which Indian fashion in night clothes admits. In the opposite corner near the window, which was closed, Parker was stretched at full length upon his back. Yellow Bear was stone dead, while the quick gasps of his companion indicated that he was in but a stone's throw of eternity. The chief was removed to the bed, and through the untiring efforts of Drs. Beall and Moore his life has been saved.

"Finding Quanah sufficiently able to converse, the reporter of the *Gazette* questioned him as to the cause of the unhappy occurrence, and elicited the following facts:

" 'I came,' said the chief, 'into the room about midnight, and found Yellow Bear in bed. I lit the gas myself. I smelt no gas when I came into the room. When I went to bed I turned the gas off. I did not blow it out. After a while I smelt the gas, but went to sleep. I woke up and shook Yellow Bear and told him 'I'm mighty sick and hurting all over.' Yellow Bear says, 'I'm mighty sick, too.' I got up, and fell down and all around the room, and that's all I know about it.'

" 'Why didn't you open the door?' asked the reporter.

" 'I was too crazy to know anything,' replied the chief.   *   *   *   *   *

"It is indeed, a source of congratulation that the chief will recover, as otherwise his tribe could not be made to understand the occurrence, and results detrimental to those having interests in the Territory would inevitably follow."

The new town of Quanah, in Hardeman county, Texas, was named in honor of chief Quanah Parker.

We will now conclude our little work by appending the following letter, which gives a true pen portrait of the celebrated chief as he appears at his home on the "reservation:"

"ANADARKO, I. T., Feb. 4, 1886.

"* * * *

"* * * *

"We visited Quanah in his teepe. He is a fine specimen of physical manhood, tall, muscular—as straight as an arrow; gray, look-you-straight-through-the-eyes, very dark skin, perfect teeth, and a heavy, raven-black hair—the envy of feminine hearts—he wears hanging in two rolls wrapped around with red cloth. His hair is parted in the middle; the scalp-lock is a portion of hair the size of a dollar, plaited and tangled, signifying: 'If you want fight you can have it.'

"Quanah is how camped with a thousand of his subjects at the foot of some hills near Anadarko. Their white teepes, and the inmates dressed in their bright blankets and feathers, cattle grazing, children playing, lent a wierd charm to the lonely, desolate hills, lately devastated by prairie fire.   *   *   *   *

"He has three squaws, his favorite being the daughter of Yellow Bear, who met his death by asphyxiation at Fort Worth in December last. He said he gave seventeen horses for her. His daughter Cynthia, named for her grandmother, Cynthia Parker, is an inmate of the Indian Agent's house. Quanah was attired in a full suit of buck-skin tunic, leggins and moccasins elaborately trimmed in beads—a red breech-cloth, with ornamental ends hanging down. A very handsome and expensive Mexican blanket was thrown around his body; in his ears were little stuffed birds. His hair done with the feathers of bright plumaged birds. He was handsomer by far than any Ingomar the writer has ever seen—but there was no squaw fair enough to personate his Parthenia. His general aspect, manners, bearing, education, natural intelligence, show plainly that white blood trickles through his veins. When traveling he assumes a complete civilian's outfit—dude collar, watch and chain—takes out his ear-rings—he of course cannot cut off his long hair, saying that he could no longer be 'big chief.' He has a handsome carriage; drives a pair of matched grays, always traveling with one of his squaws (to do the chores). Minna-a-ton-ccha is with him now. She knows no English, but while her lord is conversing, gazes, dumb with admiration, at 'my lord'—ready to obey his slightest wish or command."

www.ingramcontent.com/pod-product-compliance
Lightning Source LLC
Chambersburg PA
CBHW020048030726
47499CB00007B/2646